O Blessed Host
Have Mercy on Us!

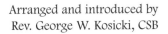

Arranged and introduced by
Rev. George W. Kosicki, CSB

O Blessed Host
Have Mercy on Us!

The Holy Eucharist in the
Diary of St. Maria Faustina Kowalska

MARIAN PRESS
STOCKBRIDGE MA 01263

2006

Available from: Marian Helpers Center Stockbridge, MA 01263

Prayerline: 1-899-804-3823
Orderline: 1-800-462-7426
Website: www.marian.org

Copy Editor: Dave Came
Typesetting & Proofreading for Original Edition:
Mary Ellen McDonald
Current Cover & Page Design: Catherine M. LeVesque
Front Cover and Title Page: Stained-glass window in the parish
church of St. Faustina's hometown of Swinice Warckie, Poland.
All world rights reserved. Reprinted with permission.
Page Design: Stained-glass window used from
the same source as above.

For texts from the English Edition of the
Diary of Saint Faustina Kowalska

NIHIL OBSTAT:
† George H. Pearce, SM
Former Archbishop of Suva, Fiji

IMPRIMATUR:
† Joseph F. Maguire
Bishop of Springfield, MA
April 9, 1984

The NIHIL OBSTAT and IMPRIMATUR are a declaration that
a book or pamphlet is considered to be free from doctrinal or moral
error. It is not implied that those who have granted the NIHIL
OBSTAT and IMPRIMATUR agree with the contents, opinions,
or statements expressed.

Note to the reader: The full religious name of St. Faustina Kowalska
was Sister Maria Faustina of the Most Blessed Sacrament. In the
world, she was known as Helen Kowalska.

Library of Congress Catalog Card Number: 2005936828
ISBN:1-59614-150-6

Printed in the United States of America by the Marian Press

I long for each Holy Communion.

— St. Faustina

Table of Contents

Preface

In this book, *O Blessed Host, Have Mercy On Us!*, Fr. George Kosicki, CSB, gathers together and organizes the texts on the Holy Eucharist found in the *Diary of St. Maria Faustina Kowalska*. The various texts are grouped with a short commentary to help you grow in your devotion to Jesus, The Divine Mercy, in the Holy Eucharist.

Our Lord's words are in boldface and St. Maria Faustina's words are in regular type. The numbers in parentheses correspond with the paragraph numbers found in the margins of the *Diary*.

You may want to bring this book with you to Holy Mass or use it during times of Adoration before the Blessed Sacrament. "O Blessed Host, have mercy on us!"

Introduction

The most solemn moment of my life is the moment when I receive Holy Communion. I long for each Holy Communion, and for every Holy Communion I give thanks to the Most Holy Trinity (Diary, 1804).

  Sister Maria Faustina of the Most Blessed Sacrament is the full name of Saint Faustina. The Holy Eucharist was the center and key to her life. Almost every page of her *Diary* makes a reference to the Eucharist.

Repeatedly, she is awed by the mystery of mercy in the Eucharist:

O what awesome mysteries take place during Mass! One day we will know what God is preparing for us in each Mass, and what sort of gift He is preparing in it for us (Diary, 914).

May your devotion to the Eucharist increase as you regularly, even daily, reflect on the words of the *Diary of Saint Faustina* — and may Holy Communion become for you "the most solemn moment" of your life.

Yearly Patron

How Saint Faustina rejoiced when her secret desire was fulfilled again and again as she drew by lot her New Year's Patron: "The Most Blessed Eucharist":

There is a custom among us of drawing by lot, on New Year's Day, special Patrons for ourselves for the whole year. In the morning during meditation, there arose within me a secret desire that the Eucharistic Jesus be my special Patron for this year also, as in the past. But, hiding this desire from my Beloved, I spoke to Him about everything else but that. When we came to refectory for breakfast, we blessed ourselves and began drawing our patrons. When I approached the holy cards on which the names of the patrons were written, without hesitation I took one, but I didn't read the name immediately as I wanted to mortify myself for a few minutes. Suddenly, I heard a voice in my soul: **I am your**

patron. Read. I looked at once at the inscription and read, "Patron for the Year 1935 — the Most Blessed Eucharist." My heart leapt with joy, and I slipped quietly away from the sisters and went for a short visit before the Blessed Sacrament, where I poured out my heart. But Jesus sweetly admonished me that I should be at that moment together with the sisters. I went immediately in obedience to the rule (*Diary*, 360).

Amen.

Greatest Gift

*Saint Faustina describes the
Holy Eucharist as the Lord's greatest gift.
What great majesty is present!*

During Mass, I thanked the Lord Jesus for having deigned to redeem us and for having given us that greatest of all gifts; namely, His love in Holy Communion; that is, His very own Self. At that moment, I was drawn into the bosom of the Most Holy Trinity, and I was immersed in the love of the Father, the Son, and the Holy Spirit. These moments are hard to describe (*Diary*, 1670).

When I was attending Mass in a certain church with another sister, I felt the greatness and majesty of God; I felt the church was permeated by God. His majesty enveloped me and, though it terrified me, it filled me with peace and joy. I knew that nothing could oppose His will. Oh, if only all souls knew who is living in our churches, there would not be so many outrages and so much disrespect in these holy places! (*Diary*, 409).

Amen.

Cenacle

During a Holy Hour of Adoration, in a vision of the Cenacle, Saint Faustina saw the institution of the Holy Eucharist. She came to understand profoundly the mystery of the Eucharist and the Lord's great humility:

Holy Hour — Thursday. During this hour of prayer, Jesus allowed me to enter the Cenacle, and I was a witness to what happened there. However, I was most deeply moved when, before the Consecration, Jesus raised His eyes to heaven and entered into a mysterious conversation with His Father. It is only in eternity that we shall really understand that moment. His eyes were like two flames; His face was radiant, white as snow; His whole personage full of majesty, His soul full of longing. At the moment of Consecration, love rested satiated — the sacrifice fully consummated. Now only the external ceremony of death will be carried out — external destruction; the essence [of it] is in the Cenacle. Never in my whole life had I understood this mystery so profoundly as during that Hour of Adoration. Oh, how ardently I desire that the whole world would come to know this unfathomable mystery! (*Diary*, 684).

During Mass today, I saw the Lord Jesus, who said to me, **Be at peace, My daughter; I see your efforts, which are very pleasing to Me.** And the Lord disappeared, and it was time for Holy Communion. After I received Holy Communion, I suddenly saw the Cenacle and in it Jesus and the Apostles. I saw the institution of the Most Blessed Sacrament. Jesus allowed me to penetrate His interior, and I came to know the greatness of His majesty and, at the same time, His great humbling of Himself. The extraordinary light that allowed me to see His majesty revealed to me, at the same time, what was in my own soul (*Diary*, 757).

Amen.

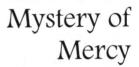

Mystery of Mercy

Saint Faustina expressed the depth of the mystery of the Holy Eucharist as a mystery of mercy:

Who will ever conceive and understand the depth of mercy that has gushed forth from Your Heart? (*Diary*, 832).

It is only in eternity that we shall know the great mystery effected in us by Holy Communion. O most precious moments of my life! (*Diary*, 840).

Oh, what awesome mysteries take place during Mass! A great mystery is accomplished in the Holy Mass. With what great devotion should we listen to and take part in this death of Jesus. One day we will know what God is doing for us in each Mass, and what sort of gift He is preparing in it for us. Only His divine love could permit that such a gift be provided for us. O Jesus, my Jesus, with what great pain is my soul pierced when I see this fountain of life gushing forth with such sweetness and power for each soul, while at the same time I see souls withering away and drying up through their own fault. O Jesus, grant that the power of mercy embrace these souls (*Diary*, 914).

Jesus, there is one more secret in my life, the deepest and dearest to my heart: it is You Yourself when You come to my heart under the appearance of bread. Herein lies the whole secret of my sanctity. Here my heart is so united with Yours as to be but one. There are no more secrets, because all that is Yours is mine, and all that is mine is Yours. Such is the omnipotence and the miracle of Your mercy. All the tongues of men and of angels united could not find words adequate to this mystery of Your love and mercy (*Diary*, 1489).

Amen.

Transform Me

A very special aspect of Saint Faustina's life was her desire and prayer to be transformed into a living host, a wafer, hidden and broken to be given to others:

Make of me, Jesus, a pure and agreeable offering before the Face of Your Father. Jesus, transform me, miserable and sinful as I am, into Your own self (for You can do all things), and give me to Your Eternal Father. I want to become a sacrificial host before You, but an ordinary wafer to people. I want the fragrance of my sacrifice to be known to You alone. O Eternal God, an unquenchable fire of supplication for Your mercy burns within me. I know and understand that this is my task, here and in eternity. You Yourself have told me to speak about this great mercy and about Your goodness (*Diary*, 483).

Oh, what joy it is to empty myself for the sake of immortal souls! I know that the grain of wheat must be destroyed and ground between millstones in order to become food. In the same way, I must become destroyed in order to be useful to the Church and souls, even though exteriorly no one will notice my sacrifice. O Jesus, outwardly I want to be hidden, just like this little wafer wherein the eye perceives nothing, and yet I am a host consecrated to You (*Diary*, 641).

O Jesus, how sorry I feel for poor sinners. Jesus, grant them contrition and repentance. Remember Your own sorrowful Passion. I know Your infinite mercy and cannot bear it that a soul that has cost You so much should perish. Jesus, give me the souls of sinners; let Your mercy rest upon them. Take everything away from me, but give me souls. I want to become a sacrificial host for sinners. Let the shell of my body conceal my offering, for Your Most Sacred Heart is also hidden in a Host, and certainly You are a living sacrifice.

Transform me into Yourself, O Jesus, that I may be a living sacrifice and pleasing to You. I desire to atone at each moment for poor sinners. The sacrifice of my spirit is hidden under the veil of the body; the human eye does not perceive it, and for that reason it is pure and pleasing to You. O my Creator and Father of great mercy, I trust in You, for You are Goodness Itself. Souls, do not be afraid of God, but trust in Him, for He is good, and His mercy is everlasting (*Diary*, 908).

Most sweet Jesus, set on fire my love for You and transform me into Yourself. Divinize me that my deeds may be pleasing to You. May this be accomplished by the power of the Holy Communion which I receive daily. Oh, how greatly I desire to be wholly transformed into You, O Lord! (*Diary*, 1289).

I am a host in Your hand, Jesus. Make use of me so that You may enter into sinners Yourself. Demand anything You like; no sacrifice will seem too much for me when souls are at stake (*Diary*, 1622).

When I had received Jesus in Holy Communion, my heart cried out with all its might, "Jesus, transform me into another host! I want to be a living host for You. You are a great and all-powerful Lord; You can grant me this favor." And the Lord answered me, **You are a living host, pleasing to the Heavenly Father. But reflect: What is a host? A sacrifice. And so ... ?**

O my Jesus, I understand the meaning of "host," the meaning of sacrifice. I desire to be before Your Majesty a living host; that is, a living sacrifice that daily burns in Your honor (*Diary*, 1826).

Amen.

All Good

Saint Faustina felt this call to be transformed into a living host as a "holy fire." It was the great moment of her life:

All the good that is in me is due to Holy Communion. I owe everything to it. I feel that this holy fire has transformed me completely. Oh, how happy I am to be a dwelling place for You, O Lord! My heart is a temple in which You dwell continually ... (*Diary*, 1392).

The most solemn moment of my life is the moment when I receive Holy Communion. I long for each Holy Communion, and for every Holy Communion I give thanks to the Most Holy Trinity.

If the angels were capable of envy, they would envy us for two things: one is the receiving of Holy Communion, and the other is suffering (*Diary*, 1804).

Amen.

A ll the good that is
in me is due to
Holy Communion
(Diary, 1392).

Bridal Union

*The experience of being a living host,
chosen, blessed, broken, and given was the
central experience of Saint Faustina's life.
But this experience was based on her union
of love with the living God. This union
was most profoundly experienced in
conjunction with the Holy Eucharist, either
during Mass and Holy Communion, or
during adoration of the Blessed Sacrament.
Her union with the Lord was,
in His words, as a bride:*

Now you shall consider.
**My love in the Blessed Sacrament.
Here, I am entirely yours, soul, body
and divinity, as your Bridegroom. You
know what love demands: one thing
only, reciprocity ...** (*Diary*, 1770).

When I received Holy Communion,
I said to Him, "Jesus, I thought about
You so many times last night," and Jesus
answered me, **And I thought of you**

before I called you into being. "Jesus, in what way were You thinking about me?" **In terms of admitting you to My eternal happiness.** After these words, my soul was flooded with the love of God. I could not stop marveling at how much God loves us (*Diary*, 1292).

Today, I am preparing myself for Your coming as a bride does for the coming of her bridegroom. He is a great Lord, this Bridegroom of mine. The heavens cannot contain Him. The Seraphim who stand closest to Him cover their faces and repeat unceasingly: Holy, Holy, Holy (*Diary*, 1805).

We know each other mutually, O Lord, in the dwelling of my heart. Yes, now it is I who am receiving you as a Guest in the little home of my heart, but the time is coming when You will call me to Your dwelling place, which You have prepared for me from the beginning of the world. Oh, what am I compared to You, O Lord? (*Diary*, 909).

Amen.

Strength and Support

Holy Communion was the strength and support of Saint Faustina in her daily struggle. The Lord taught her: "In the Host is your power; it will defend you." She said that the Eucharist was her strength from her tender years:

Hidden Jesus, in You lies all my strength. From my most tender years, the Lord Jesus in the Blessed Sacrament has attracted me to Himself. Once, when I was seven years old, at a Vesper Service, conducted before the Lord Jesus in the monstrance, the love of God was imparted to me for the first time and filled my little heart; and the Lord gave me understanding of divine things. From that day until this, my love for the hidden God has been growing constantly to the point of closest intimacy. All the strength of my soul flows from the Blessed

Sacrament. I spend all my free moments in conversation with Him. He is my Master (*Diary*, 1404).

O my Jesus, You alone know what persecutions I suffer, and this only because I am being faithful to You and following Your orders. You are my strength; sustain me that I may always carry out what You ask of me.

Of myself I can do nothing, but when You sustain me, all difficulties are nothing for me. O my Lord, I can see very well that from the time when my soul first received the capacity to know You, my life has been a continual struggle which has become increasingly intense.

Every morning during meditation, I prepare myself for the whole day's struggle. Holy Communion assures me that I will win the victory; and so it is. I fear the day when I do not receive Holy Communion. This Bread of the Strong gives me all the strength I need to carry on my mission and the courage to do whatever the Lord asks of me. The courage and strength that are in me are not of me, but of Him who lives in me — it is the Eucharist.

O my Jesus, the misunderstandings are so great; sometimes, were it not for the Eucharist, I would not have the courage to go any further along the way You have marked out for me (*Diary*, 91).

On Thursday, when I went to my cell, I saw over me the Sacred Host in great brightness. Then I heard a voice that seemed to be coming from above the Host: **In the Host is your power; it will defend you.** After these words, the vision disappeared, but a strange power entered my soul, and a strange light as to what our love for God consists in; namely, in doing His will (*Diary*, 616).

December 12, [1936]. Today, I only received Holy Communion and stayed for a few moments of the Mass. All my strength is in You, O Living Bread. It would be difficult for me to live through the day if I did not receive Holy Communion. It is my shield; without You, Jesus, I know not how to live (*Diary*, 814).

I find myself so weak that were it not for Holy Communion I would fall continually. One thing alone sustains me, and that is Holy Communion. From it I draw my strength; in it is all my comfort.

I fear life on days when I do not receive Holy Communion. I fear my own self. Jesus concealed in the Host is everything to me. From the tabernacle I draw strength, power, courage and light. Here, I seek consolation in time of anguish. I would not know how to give glory to God if I did not have the Eucharist in my heart (*Diary*, 1037).

When I had received Jesus in Holy Communion, my heart cried out with all its might, "Jesus, transform me into another host! I want to be a living host for You. You are a great and all-powerful Lord; You can grant me this favor." And the Lord answered me, **You are a living host, pleasing to the Heavenly Father. But reflect: What is a host? A sacrifice. And so ... ?**

O my Jesus, I understand the meaning of "host," the meaning of sacrifice. I desire to be before Your Majesty a living host; that is, a living sacrifice that daily burns in Your honor.

When my strength begins to fail, it is Holy Communion that will sustain me and give me strength. Indeed, I fear the day on which I would not receive Holy Communion. My soul draws astonishing strength from Holy Communion (*Diary*, 1826).

Amen.

Offering

Saint Faustina placed herself on the paten and in the chalice, offering herself in union with Jesus for the salvation of souls:

I will spend all my free moments at the feet of [Our Lord in] the Blessed Sacrament. At the feet of Jesus, I will seek light, comfort, and strength. I will show my gratitude unceasingly to God for His great mercy towards me, never forgetting the favors He has bestowed on me, especially the grace of a vocation (*Diary*, 224).

I will enclose myself in the chalice of Jesus so that I may comfort Him continually. I will do everything within my power to save souls, and I will do it through prayer and suffering.

I try always to be a Bethany for Jesus, so that He may rest here after all His labors. In Holy Communion, my union with Jesus is so intimate and incomprehensible that even if I wanted to describe it in writing I could not do so, because I lack the words (*Diary*, 735).

Amen.

Experience of Presence

Saint Faustina tells us that she often experienced the presence of the Lord after Holy Communion and that she found it continued throughout the day:

I often feel God's presence after Holy Communion in a special and tangible way. I know God is in my heart. And the fact that I feel Him in my heart does not interfere with my duties. Even when I am dealing with very important matters which require attention, I do not lose the presence of God in my soul, and I am closely united with Him. With Him I go to work, with Him I go for recreation, with Him I suffer, with Him I rejoice; I live in Him and He in me. I am never alone, because He is my constant companion. He is present to me at every moment. Our intimacy is very close, through a union of blood and of life (*Diary*, 318).

Often during Mass, I see the Lord in my soul;
I feel His presence which pervades my being. I
sense His divine gaze; I have long talks with
Him without saying a word; I know what His
divine Heart desires, and I always do what will
please Him the most. I love Him to distraction,
and I feel that I am being loved by God. At those
times when I meet with God deep within myself,
I feel so happy that I do not know how to express it.
Such moments are short, for the soul could not bear
it for long, as separation from the body would be
inevitable. Though these moments are very short,
their power, however, which is transmitted to the
soul, remains with it for a very long time. Without
the least effort, I experience the profound
recollection which then envelops me — and it
does not diminish even if I talk with people, nor
does it interfere with the performance of my duties.
I feel the constant presence of God without any
effort of my soul. I know that I am united with
Him as closely as a drop of water is united with the
bottomless ocean (*Diary*, 411).

Once after Holy Communion, I heard these words:
You are Our dwelling place. At that moment, I felt

in my soul the presence of the Holy Trinity, the Father, the Son, and the Holy Spirit. I felt that I was the temple of God. I felt I was a child of the Father. I cannot explain all this, but the spirit understands it well. O infinite Goodness, how low You stoop to Your miserable creature! (*Diary*, 451).

Amen.

Our intimacy
is very close,
through a union
of blood and life
(Diary, 318).

Continuous Presence

A special Christmas gift was given to Saint Faustina of continuous presence of the Eucharist from one Holy Communion until the next:s:

Midnight Mass. During Holy Mass, I again saw the little Infant Jesus, extremely beautiful, joyfully stretching out His little arms to me. After Holy Communion, I heard the words: I am always in your heart; not only when you receive Me in Holy Communion, but always. I spent these holy days in great joy (*Diary*, 575).

After Holy Communion, I felt the beating of the Heart of Jesus in my own heart. Although I have been aware, for a long time, that Holy Communion continues in me until the next Communion, today — and throughout the whole day — I am adoring Jesus in my heart and asking Him, by His grace, to protect little children from the evil that threatens them. A vivid and even physically felt presence of God continues throughout the day and does not in the least interfere with my duties (*Diary*, 1821).

Amen.

Visions of Jesus

Saint Faustina regularly experienced the visions of the Lord Jesus during Holy Mass. Over sixty such versions are recorded in her Diary, mostly of the infant Jesus, a few occasions with the Blessed Mother, at other times of Jesus during His passion, and at times of His majesty. Some dozen times, she records seeing the rays of mercy as in the image of the Merciful Savior coming from the Holy Eucharist, at times covering the world:

Low Sunday; that is, the Feast of The Divine Mercy, the conclusion of the Jubilee of Redemption. When we went to take part in the celebrations, my heart leapt with joy that the two solemnities were so closely united. I asked God for mercy on the souls of sinners. Toward the end of the service, when the priest took the Blessed Sacrament to bless the people, I saw the

Lord Jesus as He is represented in the image. The Lord gave His blessing, and the rays extended over the whole world (*Diary*, 420).

Once, the image was being exhibited over the altar during the Corpus Christi procession [June 20, 1935]. When the priest exposed the Blessed Sacrament, and the choir began to sing, the rays from the image pierced the Sacred Host and spread out all over the world. Then I heard these words: **These rays of mercy will pass through you, just as they have passed through this Host, and they will go out through all the world.** At these words, profound joy invaded my soul (*Diary*, 441).

On Friday during Mass when my soul was flooded with God's happiness, I heard these words in my soul: **My mercy has passed into souls through the divine-human Heart of Jesus as a ray from the sun passes through crystal.** I felt in my heart and understood that every approach to God is brought about by Jesus, in Him and through Him (*Diary*, 528).

I saw how the two rays, as painted in the image, issued from the Host and spread over the whole world. This lasted only a moment, but it seemed as though it had lasted all day, and our chapel was overcrowded all day long, and the whole day abounded in joy (*Diary*, 1046).

Today, when the chaplain [Father Theodore] brought the Lord Jesus, a light issued from the Host, its light striking my heart and filling me with a great fire of love. Jesus was letting me know that I should answer the inspirations of grace with more faithfulness, and that my vigilance should be more subtle (*Diary*, 1462).

During Holy Mass, I saw the Infant Jesus in the chalice, and He said to me, **I am dwelling in your heart as you see Me in this chalice** (*Diary*, 1820).

Amen.

I ask God for mercy on the souls of sinner (Diary, 420).

Time of Teaching

The Holy Eucharist was a precious time of teaching for Saint Faustina. Our Lord Jesus taught her how to live a spiritual life and about her mission of winning souls.

During Holy Hour today, I asked the Lord Jesus if He would deign to teach me about the spiritual life, Jesus answered me, **My daughter, faithfully live up to the words which I speak to you. Do not value any external thing too highly, even if it were to seem very precious to you. Let go of yourself, and abide with Me continually. Entrust everything to Me and do nothing on your own, and you will always have great freedom of spirit. No circumstances or events will ever be able to upset you. Set little store on what people say. Let everyone judge you as they like. Do not make excuses for yourself, — it will do** you no harm. Give away everything at the first sign of a demand, even if they were the most necessary things. Do not ask for anything without consulting Me. Allow them to take away even what is due you — respect, your good name — let your spirit rise above all that. And so, set free from everything, rest close to My Heart, not allowing your peace to be disturbed by anything. **My pupil, consider the words which I have spoken to you** (*Diary*, 1685).

After Holy Communion today, Jesus said, **My daughter give Me souls. Know that it is your mission to win souls for Me by prayer and sacrifice, and by encouraging them to trust in My mercy** (*Diary*, 1690).

Amen.

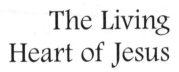

The Living Heart of Jesus

Saint Faustina describes the living Heart of Jesus present in the Eucharist:

O Living Host, my one and only strength, fountain of love and mercy, embrace the whole world, fortify faint souls. Oh, blessed be the instant and the moment when Jesus left us His most merciful Heart! (*Diary*, 223).

As I was praying to the living Heart of Jesus in the Blessed Sacrament for the intention of a certain priest, Jesus suddenly gave me knowledge of His goodness and said to me, **I will give him nothing that is beyond his strength** (*Diary*, 1607).

Amen.

O Living Host, my one and only strength, fountain of love and mercy (Diary, 223).

Doubt

*Saint Faustina records two occasions
when she doubted her worthiness to receive
Holy Communion. The Lord clearly corrects her:*

Once, I desired very much to receive Holy Communion, but I had a certain doubt, and I did not go. I suffered greatly because of this. It seemed to me that my heart would burst from the pain. When I set about my work, my heart full of bitterness, Jesus suddenly stood by me and said, **My daughter, do not omit Holy Communion unless you know well that your fall was serious; apart from this, no doubt must stop you from uniting yourself with Me in the mystery of My love. Your minor faults will disappear in My love like a piece of straw thrown into a great furnace. Know that you grieve Me much when you fail to receive Me in Holy Communion** (*Diary*, 156).

One time, I was in doubt as to whether what had happened to me had seriously offended the Lord Jesus or not. As I could not solve this doubt, I made up my mind not to go to Communion before first going to confession, although I immediately made an act of contrition, as it is my habit to ask for forgiveness after the slightest transgression. During those days when I did not receive Holy Communion, I did not feel the presence of God. This caused me unspeakable pain, but I took it as a punishment for sin. However, at the time of Holy Confession I was reproached for not going to Holy Communion, because what had happened to me was not an obstacle to receiving Holy Communion. After confession, I received Holy Communion, and I saw the Lord Jesus who said to me, **Know, my daughter, that you caused Me more sorrow by not uniting yourself with Me in Holy Communion than you did by that small transgression** (*Diary*, 612).

Amen.

Chaplet

The Divine Mercy Chaplet that our Lord taught Saint Faustina is an offering of the Holy Eucharist that extends the offering of Holy Mass. It is eminently Eucharistic:

Whe hen I enter chapel, I heard these words interiorly: **Every time you enter the chapel, immediately recite the prayer which I taught you yesterday.** When I had said the prayer, in my soul I heard these words:

This prayer will serve to appease My wrath. You will recite it for nine days, on the beads of the rosary, in the following manner: First of all, you will say one OUR FATHER and HAIL MARY and the I BELIEVE IN GOD. Then on the OUR FATHER beads you will say the following words: "Eternal Father, I offer You the Body and Blood, Soul and Divinity of Your dearly beloved Son, Our Lord Jesus Christ, in atonement of

our sins and those of the whole world." On the HAIL MARY beads you will say the following words: "For the sake of His sorrowful Passion have mercy on us and on the whole world."

In conclusion, three times you will recite these words: "Holy God, Holy Mighty One, Holy Immortal One, have mercy on us and on the whole world" (*Diary*, 476).

Amen.

Mercy Sunday

Divine Mercy Sunday, one of the main revelations to Saint Faustina, is centered on the worthy reception of Holy Communion — which our Lord calls "the Fount of My Mercy."

On one occasion, I heard these words: **My daughter, tell the whole world about My inconceivable mercy. I desire that the Feast of Mercy be a refuge and shelter for all souls, and especially for poor sinners. On that day the very depths of My tender mercy are open. I pour out a whole ocean of graces upon those souls who approach the Fount of My Mercy. The soul that will go to Confession and receive Holy Communion shall obtain complete forgiveness of sins and punishment. On that day all the divine floodgates through which graces flow are opened. Let no soul fear to draw near to Me, even though its sins be as scarlet. My** mercy is so great that no mind, be it of man or of angel, will be able to fathom it throughout all eternity. Everything that exists has come forth from the very depths of My most tender mercy. Every soul in its relation to Me will contemplate My love and mercy throughout eternity. The Feast of Mercy emerged from My very depths of tenderness. It is My desire that it be solemnly celebrated on the first Sunday after Easter. Mankind will not have peace until it turns to the Fount of My Mercy (*Diary*, 699).

Amen.

Passion of Jesus

Saint Faustina experienced the Passion of Jesus in her own body, during Holy Mass:

When I experienced these sufferings for the first time, it was like this: after the annual vows, on a certain day, during prayer, I saw a great brilliance and, issuing from the brilliance, rays which completely enveloped me. Then suddenly, I felt a terrible pain in my hands, my feet, and my side and the thorns of the crown of thorns. I experienced these sufferings during Holy Mass on Friday, but this was only for a brief moment. This was repeated for several Fridays, and later on I did not experience any sufferings up to the present time; that is, up to the end of September of this year. In the course of the present illness, during Holy Mass one Friday, I felt myself pierced by the same sufferings, and this has been repeated on every Friday and sometimes when I meet a soul that is not in the state of grace. Although this is infrequent, and the suffering lasts a very short time, still it is terrible, and I would not be able to bear it without a special grace from God. There is no outward indication of these sufferings. What will come later, I do not know. All this, for the sake of souls (*Diary*, 759).

I could not assist at the whole Mass today; I assisted at only the most important parts, and after receiving Holy Communion I immediately returned to my solitude. The presence of God suddenly enveloped me, and at the same moment I felt the Passion of the Lord, for a very short while. During that moment, I attained a more profound knowledge of the work of mercy (*Diary*, 808).

I have offered this day for priests. I have suffered more today than ever before, both interiorly and exteriorly. I did not know it was possible to suffer so much in one day. I tried to make a Holy Hour, in the course of which my spirit had a taste of the bitterness of the Garden of Gethsemane. I am fighting alone, supported by His arm, against all the difficulties that face me like unassailable walls. But I trust in the power of His name and I fear nothing (*Diary*, 823).

During Holy Mass, I saw the Lord Jesus nailed upon the cross amidst great torments. A soft moan issued from His Heart. After some time, He said, **I thirst. I thirst for the salvation of souls. Help Me, My daughter, to save souls. Join your sufferings to My Passion and offer them to the heavenly Father for sinners** (*Diary*, 1032).

Monday of Holy Week. I asked the Lord to let me take part in His Sorrowful Passion that I might experience in soul and body, to the extent that this is possible for a creature, His bitter Passion. I asked to experience all the bitterness, in so far as this was possible. And the Lord answered that He would give me this grace, and that on Thursday, after Holy Communion, He would grant this in a special way (*Diary*, 1034).

Amen.

The presence of God suddenly enveloped me, and at the same moment I felt the Passion of the Lord (Diary, 808).

Desire of Saint Faustina

The ardor of Saint Faustina's desire for Holy Communion pleased the Lord. He even sent a seraph angel to bring her Communion:

When I received Holy Communion, I said to Him, "Jesus, I thought about You so many times last night," and Jesus answered me, **And I thought of you before I called you into being.** "Jesus, in what way were You thinking about me?" **In terms of admitting you to My eternal happiness.** After these words, my soul was flooded with the love of God. I could not stop marveling at how much God loves us (*Diary*, 1292).

After Holy Communion the Lord said to me, **If the priest had not brought Me to you, I would have come Myself under the same species. My daughter, your**

sufferings of this night obtained the grace of mercy for an immense number of souls (*Diary*, 1459). Jesus said to me, **Be at peace; I am with you.** Tired, I fell asleep. In the evening, the sister [Sister David] who was to look after me came and said, "Tomorrow you will not receive the Lord Jesus, Sister, because you are very tired; later on, we shall see." This hurt me very much, but I said with great calmness, "Very well," and, resigning myself totally to the will of the Lord, I tried to sleep.

In the morning, I made my meditation and prepared for Holy Communion, even though I was not to receive the Lord Jesus. When my love and desire had reached a high degree, I saw at my bedside a Seraph, who gave me Holy Communion, saying these words: "Behold, the Lord of Angels." When I received the Lord, my spirit was drowned in the love of God and in amazement. This was repeated for thirteen days, although I was never sure he would bring me Holy Communion the next day. Yet, I put my trust completely in the goodness of God, but did not even dare to think that I would receive Holy Communion in this way on the following day.

The Seraph was surrounded by a great light, the divinity and love of God being reflected in him. He wore a golden robe and, over it, a transparent surplice and a transparent stole. The chalice was crystal, covered with a transparent veil. As soon as he gave me the Lord, he disappeared (*Diary*, 1676).

Today, I feel an abyss of misery in my soul. I want to approach Holy Communion as a fountain of mercy and to drown myself completely in this ocean of love. When I received Jesus, I threw myself into Him as into an abyss of unfathomable mercy. And the more I felt I was misery itself, the stronger grew my trust in Him (*Diary*, 1817).

Today, when the doctor [Adam Silberg] making his rounds came to see me, he somehow didn't like the way I looked. Naturally, I was suffering more, and so my temperature had gone up considerably. Consequently, he decided I must not go down for Holy Communion until my temperature dropped to normal. I said, "All right," although pain seized my heart; but I said I would go only if I had no fever. So he agreed to that. When the doctor left, I said to the Lord, "Jesus, now it is up to You whether I shall go or not," and I didn't think about it anymore, although the thought kept coming to my mind: I am not to have Jesus — no, that's impossible — and not just once but for several days, until my temperature drops. But in the evening, I said to the Lord, "Jesus, if my Communions are pleasing to You, I beg You humbly, grant that I have not one degree of fever tomorrow morning."

In the morning, as I was taking my temperature, I thought to myself, "If there is even one degree, I will not get up because that would be contrary to obedience." But when I looked at the thermometer, there wasn't even one degree of fever. I jumped to my feet at once and went to Holy Communion. When the doctor came and I told him that I had had not even one degree of fever, and so had gone to Holy Communion, he was surprised. I begged him not to make it difficult for me to go to Holy Communion, for it would have an adverse effect on the treatment. The doctor answered, "For peace of conscience and at the same time to avoid difficulties for yourself, Sister, let us make the following agreement: when the weather is fine, and it isn't raining, and you feel all right, then, Sister, please go; but you must weigh these matters in your conscience." It made me very happy that the doctor was being so considerate for my sake. You see, Jesus, that I have already done whatever was up to me; now I am counting on You and am quite at peace (*Diary*, 878).

Amen.

Desire and
Pain of Jesus

Jesus desires to give Himself wholly to us in Holy Communion, but He is pained by the obstacles we place in His way:

After Communion today, Jesus told me how much He desires to come to human hearts. **I desire to unite Myself with human souls; My great delight is to unite Myself with souls. Know, My daughter, that when I come to a human heart in Holy Communion, My hands are full of all kinds of graces which I want to give to the soul. But souls do not even pay any attention to Me; they leave Me to Myself and busy themselves with other things. Oh, how sad I am that souls do not recognize Love! They treat Me as a dead object.** I answered Jesus, "O Treasure of my heart, the only object of my love and entire delight of my soul, I want to adore

You in my heart as You are adored on the throne of Your eternal glory. My love wants to make up to You at least in part for the coldness of so great a number of souls. Jesus, behold my heart which is for You a dwelling place to which no one else has entry. You alone repose in it as in a beautiful garden (*Diary*, 1385).

Oh, how painful it is to Me that souls so seldom unite themselves to Me in Holy Communion. I wait for souls, and they are indifferent toward Me. I love them tenderly and sincerely, and they distrust Me. I want to lavish My graces on them, and they do not want to accept them. They treat Me as a dead object, whereas My Heart is full of love and mercy. In order that you may know at least some of My pain, imagine the most tender of mothers who has great love for her children, while those children spurn her love. Consider her pain. No one is in a position to console her. This is but a feeble image and likeness of My love (*Diary*, 1447).

I saw how unwillingly the Lord Jesus came to certain souls in Holy Communion. And He spoke these words to me: **I enter into certain hearts as into a second Passion** (*Diary*, 1598).

Write for the benefit of religious souls that it delights Me to come to their hearts in Holy Communion. But if there is anyone else in such a heart, I cannot bear it and quickly leave that heart, taking with Me all the gifts and graces I have prepared for the soul. And the soul does not even notice My going. After some time, inner emptiness and dissatisfaction will come to her attention. Oh, if only she would turn to Me then, I would help her to cleanse her heart, and I would fulfill everything in her soul; but without her knowledge and consent, I cannot be the Master of her heart (*Diary*, 1683).

Amen.

Jesus, behold my heart which is for You a dwelling place to which no one else has entry

(Diary, 1385).

Visits

*Saint Faustina spent all her free moments
in extra visits to the Blessed Sacrament.
She asked and obtained strength
and greater love for the Lord:*

I will spend all my free
moments at the feet of [Our Lord in] the
Blessed Sacrament. At the feet of Jesus, I
will seek light, comfort, and strength. I
will show my gratitude unceasingly to
God for His great mercy towards me,
never forgetting the favors He has
bestowed on me, especially the grace
of a vocation (*Diary*, 224).

I spend every free moment at the feet of
the hidden God. He is my Master; I ask
Him about everything; I speak to Him
about everything. Here I obtain strength
and light; here I learn everything; here I
am given light on how to act toward
my neighbor. From the time I left the
novitiate, I have enclosed myself in the
tabernacle together with Jesus, my Master.
He Himself drew me into the fire of living
love on which everything converges
(*Diary*, 704).

I spend every free moment at the feet of the hidden God (Diary, 704).

Adoration

Saint Faustina records dozens of times when she spent time in adoration before the Blessed Sacrament. Adoration was a part of her personal devotion and part of the community schedule. Her experience is a marvelous teaching on making a Holy Hour of Adoration:

I recall that I have received most light during adoration which I made lying prostrate before the Blessed Sacrament for half an hour every day throughout Lent. During that time I came to know myself and God more profoundly. And yet, even though I had the superiors' permission to do so, I encountered many obstacles to praying in such a way.

Let the soul be aware that, in order to pray and persevere in prayer, one must arm oneself with patience and cope bravely with exterior and interior difficulties. The interior difficulties are discouragement, dryness, heaviness of spirit, and temptations. The exterior difficulties are human respect and time; one must observe the time set apart for prayer. This has been my personal experience because, when I did not pray at the time assigned for prayer, later on I could not do it because of my duties; or if I did manage to do so, this was only with great difficulty, because my thoughts kept wandering off to my duties. I also experienced this difficulty: when a soul has prayed well and left prayer in a state of profound interior recollection, others resist its recollection; and so, the soul must be patient to persevere in prayer. It often happened to me that when my soul was more deeply immersed in God, and I had derived greater fruit from prayer, and God's presence accompanied me during the day, and at work there was more recollection and greater precision and effort at my duty, this was precisely when I received the most rebukes for being negligent in my duty and indifferent to everything; because less recollected souls want others to be like them, for they are a constant [source of] remorse to them (*Diary*, 147).

Night adoration on Thursdays. I made my Hour of Adoration from eleven o'clock till midnight. I offered it for the conversion of hardened sinners, especially for those who have lost hope in God's mercy. I was reflecting on how much God had suffered and on how great was the love He had shown for us, and on the fact that we still do not believe that God loves us so much. O Jesus, who can understand this? What suffering it is for our Savior! How can He convince us of His love if even His death cannot convince us? I called upon the whole of heaven to join me in making amends to the Lord for the ingratitude of certain souls (*Diary*, 319).

I made an Hour of Adoration in thanksgiving for the graces which had been granted me and for my illness. Illness also is a great grace. I have been ill for four months, but I do I not recall having wasted so much as a minute of it. All has been for God and souls; I want to be faithful to Him everywhere.

During this adoration, I realized the utter care and goodness that Jesus has been lavishing upon me and the protection He has given me against all evil. I thank You especially, Jesus, for visiting me in my solitude, and I thank You also for inspiring my superiors to send me for this treatment. Give them, Jesus, the omnipotence of Your blessing and compensate them for all the losses incurred because of me (*Diary*, 1062).

Today during adoration, the Lord gave me to know how much He desires a soul to distinguish itself by deeds of love. And in spirit I saw how many souls are calling out to us, "Give us God." and the blood of the Apostles boiled up within me. I will not be stingy with it; I will shed it all to the last drop for immortal souls. Although perhaps God will not demand that in the physical sense, in spirit it is possible and no less meritorious (*Diary,* 1249).

When, during Adoration, I repeated the prayer, "Holy God" several times, a vivid presence of God suddenly swept over me, and I was caught up in spirit before the majesty of God. I saw how the Angels and the Saints of the Lord give glory to God. The glory of God is so great that I dare not try to describe it, because I would not be able to do so, and souls might think that what I have written is all there is. Saint Paul, I understand now why you did not want to describe heaven, but only said that eye has not seen, nor ear heard, nor has it entered into the heart of man what God has prepared for those who love Him (see: 1 Cor. 2:9, 2 Cor. 12: 1-7). Yes, that is indeed so. And all that has come forth from God returns to Him in the same way and gives Him perfect glory. Now I have seen the way in which I adore God; oh, how miserable it is! And what a tiny drop it is in comparison to that perfect heavenly glory. O my God, how good You are to accept my praise as well, and to turn Your Face to me with kindness and let us know that our prayer is pleasing to You (*Diary,* 1604).

Prayers and Hymns

Under God's inspiration (Diary, 1593), Saint Faustina composed prayers and hymns in honor of the Blessed Sacrament. She expressed her love, her desire, and admiration for the Eucharist so that we would grow in our love and adoration of the Lord's greatest gift. The prayer "O Blessed Host" invites the three responses suggested:

O Blessed Host, in golden chalice enclosed for me, That through the vast wilderness of exile I may pass — pure, immaculate, undefiled; Oh, grant that through the power of Your love this might come to be.

O Blessed Host, take up Your dwelling within my soul, O Thou my heart's purest love!

With Your brilliance the darkness
dispel. Refuse not Your grace to
a humble heart.

O Blessed Host, enchantment of
all heaven, though Your beauty be veiled
And captured in a crumb of bread, Strong
faith tears away that veil (*Diary*, 159).

O Blessed Host

Response:
Have mercy on us and on the whole world.

O Blessed Host, in whom is contained
the testament of God's mercy for us, and
especially for poor sinners ...

O Blessed Host, in whom is contained
the Body and Blood of the Lord Jesus as proof
of infinite mercy for us, and especially for
poor sinners ...

O Blessed Host, in whom is contained life eternal and of infinite mercy, dispensed in abundance to us and especially to poor sinners ...

O Blessed Host, in whom is contained the mercy of the Father, the Son, and the Holy Spirit toward us, and especially toward poor sinners ...

O Blessed Host, in whom is contained the infinite price of mercy which will compensate for all our debts, and especially those of poor sinners ...

O Blessed Host, in whom is contained the fountain of living water which springs from infinite mercy for us, and especially for poor sinners ...

O Blessed Host, in whom is contained the fire of purest love which blazes forth from the bosom of the Eternal Father, as from an abyss of infinite mercy for us, and especially for poor sinners ...

O Blessed Host, in whom is contained the medicine for all our infirmities, flowing from infinite mercy, as from a fount, for us and especially for poor sinners ...

O Blessed Host, in whom is contained the union between God and us through His infinite mercy for us, and especially for poor sinners ...

O Blessed Host, in whom are contained all the sentiments of the most sweet Heart of Jesus toward us, and especially poor sinners ...

Response:

We give You thanks.

O Blessed Host, our only hope in all the sufferings and adversities of life ...

O Blessed Host, our only hope in the midst of darkness and of storms within and without ...

O Blessed Host, our only hope in life
and at the hour of our death ...

O Blessed Host, our only hope in the
midst of adversities and floods of despair ...

O Blessed Host, our only hope in the
midst of falsehood and treason ...

O Blessed Host, our only hope in the
midst of the darkness and godlessness
which inundate the earth ...

O Blessed Host, our only hope in
the longing and pain in which no one will
understand us ...

O Blessed Host, our only hope
in the toil and monotony of everyday life ...

O Blessed Host, our only hope amid
the ruin of our hopes and endeavors ...

O Blessed Host, our only hope in
the midst of the ravages of the enemy and
the efforts of hell ...

Response:
I trust in You.

O Blessed Host, when the burdens
are beyond my strength and I find my efforts
are fruitless ...

O Blessed Host, when storms toss
my heart about and my fearful spirit tends
to despair ...

O Blessed Host, when my heart is
about to tremble and mortal sweat moistens
my brow ...

O Blessed Host, when everything conspires against me and black despair creeps into my soul ...

O Blessed Host, when my eyes will begin to grow dim to all temporal things and, for the first time, my spirit will behold the unknown worlds ...

O Blessed Host, when my tasks will be beyond my strength and adversity will become my daily lot ...

O Blessed Host, when the practice of virtue will appear difficult for me and my nature will grow rebellious ...

O Blessed Host, when hostile blows will be aimed against me ...

O Blessed Host, when my toils and efforts will be misjudged by others ...

O Blessed Host, when Your judgments will resound over me ... (*Diary*, 356).

All together:

O Blood and Water which gushed forth from the Heart of Jesus as a Fount of Mercy for us, I trust in You!

(Three Times.) *(Diary*, 309).

Amen.

O Merciful Jesus, how longingly You hurried to the Upper Room to consecrate the Host that I am to receive in my life. Jesus, You desired to dwell in my heart. Your living Blood unites with mine. Who can understand this close union? My heart encloses within itself the Almighty, the Infinite One. O Jesus, continue to grant me Your divine life. Let Your pure and noble Blood throb with all its might in my heart. I give You my whole being. Transform me into Yourself and make me capable of doing Your holy will in all things and of returning Your love. O my sweet Spouse, You know that my heart knows no one but You. You have opened up in my heart an insatiable depth of love for You. From the very first moment it knew You, my heart has loved You and has lost itself in You as its one and only object. May Your pure and omnipotent love be the driving force of all my actions. Who will ever conceive and understand the depth of mercy that has gushed forth from Your Heart? (*Diary*, 832).

Amen.

To stay at Your feet,
O hidden God,
Is the delight and paradise of my soul.
Here, You give me to know You,
O incomprehensible One,
And You speak to me sweetly:

**Give Me, give Me
your heart.**

Silent conversation,
alone with You, Is to experience
what heavenly beings enjoy,
And to say to God, "I will,
I will give You my heart,
O Lord," While You, O great
and incomprehensible One,
accept it graciously.

Love and sweetness
are my soul's life, And Your unceasing
presence in my soul. I live on earth
in constant rapture, And like a
Seraph I repeat, "Hosanna!"

O You Who are hidden,
body, soul, and divinity, Under the fragile
form of bread, You are my life from whom

springs an abundance of graces;
And, for me, You surpass the
delights of heaven.

When You unite Yourself
with me in Communion, O God,
I then feel my unspeakable greatness,
A greatness which flows from You,
O Lord, I humbly confess,
And despite my misery, with Your help,
I can become a saint (*Diary*, 1718).

Amen.

God's Infinite goodness in Redeeming Man

God, You could have saved thousands of worlds with one word; a single sigh from Jesus would have satisfied Your justice. But You Yourself, Jesus, purely out of love for us, underwent such a terrible Passion. Your Father's justice would have been propitiated with a single sigh from You, and all Your self-abasement is solely the work of Your mercy and Your inconceivable love. On leaving the earth, O Lord, You wanted to stay with us, and so You left us Yourself in the Sacrament of the Altar, and You opened wide Your mercy to us. There is no misery that could exhaust You; You have called us all to this fountain of love, to this spring of God's compassion. Here is the tabernacle of Your mercy, here is the remedy for all our ills. To You, O living spring of mercy, all souls are drawn; some like deer, thirsting for Your love, others to wash the wound of their sins, and still others, exhausted by life, to draw strength. At the moment of Your death on the Cross, You bestowed upon us eternal life; allowing Your most holy side to be opened, You opened an inexhaustible spring of mercy for us, giving us Your dearest possession, the Blood and Water from Your Heart. Such is the omnipotence of Your mercy. From it all grace flows to us (*Diary*, 1747).

Summary

These profound experiences and teachings during the Holy Eucharist were closely associated with the vessels of mercy: The Feast, the Image, the Chaplet, and the Three o'clock Remembrance. Reception of Holy Communion is integral to the celebration of the Feast of Divine Mercy. As said above, on a number of occasions, Saint Faustina saw the Eucharist radiate with rays like in the Image of the Merciful Savior. The Chaplet of Divine Mercy is Eucharistic. It is an offering of the Body and Blood, Soul and Divinity of the Lord Jesus Christ, to the Father, in atonement for the sins of the world. One of the devotions suggested by Our Lord to honor the hour of His death is to adore, in the Blessed Sacrament, His Heart, which is full of Mercy (see *Diary*, 1572). The vessels of mercy which the Lord gave us through Saint Faustina are Eucharistic.

The special place of the Holy Eucharist in the life of Saint Faustina can be summed up in her full official name, Sister Maria Faustina of the Most Blessed Sacrament and in the name she called herself: After her oblation, "My name is to be 'sacrifice'" (*Diary*, 135). The Lord Jesus summed up her life in what He called her:
You are a living host (*Diary*, 1826).

Her greatest desire was to be Eucharist, hidden, like Jesus, blessed by her union with the Lord, broken like Jesus in the Passion and totally given for the salvation of souls. Her prayer to be consecrated sums up her life:

> I am a white host before You,
> O Divine Priest.
> Consecrate me Yourself,
> and may my transubstantiation
> be known only to You.
> I stand before You each day as
> a sacrificial host and implore
> Your mercy upon the world (Diary, 1564).

Amen.

Practice: If possible, attend daily Mass and receive Holy Communion. Make "spiritual communions." If possible, spend some time each week in adoration before the Blessed Sacrament.

Prayer: "O Sacrament most Holy, O Sacrament Divine, all praise and all thanksgiving, be every moment Thine."

Promise: "He who eats My flesh and drinks My blood has eternal life, and I will raise him up on the last day" (Jn 6:54).

I stand before You each day as a sacrificial host and implore Your mercy upon the world (Diary, 1564).

My Favorite Prayers on the Eucharist

_____

_____

_____

_____

_____

_____

_____

_____

_____

_____

_____

_____

_____

_____

My Favorite Prayers on the Eucharist

_____

_____

_____

_____

_____

_____

_____

_____

_____

_____

_____

_____

_____

_____

_____

My Favorite Prayers on the Eucharist

_____

_____

_____

_____

_____

_____

_____

_____

_____

_____

_____

_____

_____

_____

_____

_____